SULFUR HEART

SULFUR HEART

Brooke Carter

orca soundings

ORCA BOOK PUBLISHERS

Published in Canada and the United States in 2022 by Orca Book Publishers.
orcabook.com

Library and Archives Canada Cataloguing in Publication
Title: Sulfur heart / Brooke Carter.
Names: Carter, Brooke, 1977- author.
Series: Orca soundings.
Description: Series statement: Orca soundings
Identifiers: Canadiana (print) 20210204044 | Canadiana (ebook) 20210204060 |
ISBN 9781459831605 (softcover) | ISBN 9781459831612 (PDF) |
ISBN 9781459831629 (EPUB)
Classification: LCC PS8605.A77776 S85 2022 | DDC jC813/.6—dc23

Library of Congress Control Number: 2021934073

Summary: In this high-interest accessible novel for teen readers,
Will returns home after his father is killed under mysterious circumstances.

Orca Book Publishers is committed to reducing the consumption
of nonrenewable resources in the production of our books. We make
every effort to use materials that support a sustainable future.

Orca Book Publishers gratefully acknowledges the support for its publishing
programs provided by the following agencies: the Governmentof Canada,
the Canada Council for the Arts and the Province of British Columbia
through the BC Arts Council and the Book Publishing Tax Credit.

Design by Ella Collier
Edited by Tanya Trafford
Cover photography by Getty Images/ImageegamI (front)
and Shutterstock.com/Krasovski Dmitri (back)

Printed and bound in Canada.

25 24 23 22 • 1 2 3 4

To those who dream of better places.
Go, and don't ever look back.

Chapter One

Will didn't love the big city. It wasn't home. Then again, he didn't love home either. He stared out the window of the tiny tenth-floor apartment he'd been crashing in. He thought it was like looking at an alien landscape. Home for Will was back in Hope, the armpit town he'd escaped from a couple years earlier. Hope was all mountains and landslides. It was the sulfur mill and the railyard.

When he thought of Hope, he thought of Eve. But she was always on his mind.

Where was she? Was she still afraid of the dark?

He looked at his watch. It was 5:47 in the morning. Dawn lit up the sky—an early-autumn sunrise that had no soul. Nothing but buildings, row on row, all exactly the same. Sharp edges and glinting skyscrapers. Nothing green or growing. All was clean and square and shiny.

Will drank his coffee. He hadn't slept well— but that had been true for a couple of years now. These days he had permanent dark circles under his eyes. He was the oldest eighteen-year-old on earth, and he'd only just celebrated his birthday. Here, alone, in this crappy studio apartment that didn't even belong to him. It had been two years since he'd run away, and there was hardly anything in the place to make it feel like home. A small folding table near the tiny kitchen. A phone, a newspaper, a spoon. There was no couch. No TV.

As he stared at it, the phone rang, and he jumped, sloshing hot coffee on his wrist. "Shit," he said.

He picked up the phone and paused for a moment. The caller ID said *Bro*.

He grinned as he answered it. "Hey, man, why are you calling me so early, did you have a wild night—" He fell silent and listened. Will closed his eyes as he placed his mug down on the table. It rested on the edge, close to falling off.

"What are you telling me?" he asked. He listened some more, his eyes still closed. "Yeah. I'll check it now." Will opened his eyes and then ended the call.

He opened his phone's browser and typed in *Beatty's Beat*. A flashy tabloid-style news website loaded. The top headline featured a video. Will clicked on it.

A young man with dark, curly hair appeared on-screen. "Welcome back to *Beatty's Beat*. I'm Nigel Beatty. There's been a major development. Early this morning local security guard and former cop William Homer turned up dead in a pile of sulfur at the SulCorp sulfur mill. Homer's own son left town after the mysterious death of SulCorp's chairman, Aaron Sullivan Senior. Could there be a connection? And could it have something to do with the lost Sullivan gold? So far, no one knows how Homer ended up in the sulfur. Now, in a *Beatty's Beat* exclusive, we have some visuals sent to us by an anonymous source. A warning to our viewers—this is graphic."

The broadcast cut to dark and grainy video footage of a large sulfur pile. A winch lifted a body by the feet from deep within the pile. The yellow powder slid from the corpse like fine sand.

"No!" Will cried, shutting the browser window. He braced himself against the table. The coffee cup crashed to the floor, but he made no move to clean it up. "Oh, Dad," he whispered. "I'm sorry."

Another call came through. The caller ID this time said *Aunt Justine*.

Will sighed and picked up. "Yeah," he said. "I saw the video too. My good friend let me know. Now that my dad is…I'll have to go back sooner." Will listened for a moment. "I'll call you when I get there."

He hung up and then typed a short text.

I'll be there. Wait for me.

He walked over to the single bed. His duffel bag was already packed. He pulled open the drawers of a small dresser and added some more clothes to the bag. He caught sight of himself in the mirror. "You wanted me to come back," he said softly. "You got it." He looked away.

His past had come looking for him. He'd thought he had more time. He'd thought wrong.

Chapter Two

The bus depot was all but abandoned. Will sat alone and waited until a bus labeled *Rural Route* pulled up. It was more rust than metal, and when he climbed on board a stale smell hit him full force.

The bus made its way out of the city and began a long, winding journey along a forest-edged highway. He was going home after two years away, and he didn't know what would be there when he arrived. Hell, he didn't know who *he* would be when he arrived.

Hours later the bus passed the rockslide memorial. A long time ago, several people had lost their lives under the crush of the fallen mountainside. People loved to visit to get a taste of tragedy. They loved the strange mystery of the accident. During the day, clusters of them would take pictures on the graffiti-covered rocks. But at night, when darkness fell and the moon came out, the roadside attraction lost its appeal. There were no more families picnicking on the boulders. It became what it was always meant to be—a monument to the dead.

Will loved the memorial most at night. That's when it belonged to him again and to the other locals. They were the night-walking youth.

The street kids. The hopeless ones. The rockslide was all shadow, as dark as their own thoughts and as dim as their own futures.

He imagined Eve there, sitting on the rocks, waiting for him. As the bus continued to roll along, he drifted off to sleep, her face in his mind.

———

Eve sat on a large boulder. The cliff face above was scooped out, as if sliced into by a giant ax.

All Will could do was stare at Eve. She was so pretty it hurt.

"You're so beautiful," he said.

She got up and hopped to a different boulder. She stood, arms crossed, like an ancient, sad statue.

"What, you don't want me to say you're beautiful?" he asked.

"If you knew me, you'd know how wrong that is," she said.

"I know you better than anyone," he said.

"No," she said. *"I'm a good liar. Like all the other girls who walk the highway. I can make you believe anything."*

"Not me," he said.

"Yes. You won't see until it's too late."

"Too late for what?" he asked.

"The landslide," she said. *"It comes down and crushes everything. Everyone."*

She was crying. He hated it when she cried.

"It won't crush me," he whispered.

"How do you know?" she asked.

"Because I love you."

"Then you better get out of the way," she said.

There was a loud crack, and then the mountain split in half behind her. The whole world came rushing at them.

The bus hit a pothole. Will woke with a start. He squinted against the harsh lighting of the bus interior. He'd fallen asleep with his face pressed against the grimy window.

He had arrived. Across the street was the welcome sign to the town of Hope. It used to read *WELCOME TO HOPE*, but someone had spray-painted the sign in blue paint. Now it read *WELCOME HOPELESS*.

The bus traveled into the heart of the town and down the main strip. There were a few people on the streets. Some huddled in the plywood-covered doorways of closed-up shops. The strip looked like it always had. Will had the strange thought that this was how the place would always be—frozen in time. Maybe he'd always been here. His heart hadn't left. It was still here, with Eve.

The town was dark, save for the light from the neon of bar signs and pawnshop displays.

The bus stopped to pick up a few more passengers. There were two sulfur-mill employees on their way to do the graveyard shift. Will noted their coveralls, once white but now tinted a sickly yellow from years of sulfur dust.

A woman boarded and sat in front of Will. She wore a sleeveless dress despite the chilly fall temperature. There was dark brown makeup on her arms, though Will couldn't imagine why. A small red dot—it looked like a bug—floated out from under her dress. It circled around on her upper arm before disappearing.

He leaned back in his seat.

It was midnight by the time the bus pulled up across the street from the sulfur mill. The graveyard-shift workers shuffled off. They took their time passing through the large SulCorp archway.

Will got off the bus too. He stood under that archway for a long time. He stared at the SulCorp logo, a dirty yellow image of three interconnecting pyramids.

The mill never stopped operations, especially at night. The eerie yellow glow covered the town. Most people living in Hope were employees of the mill or relatives of an employee. SulCorp had fallen onto hard times when its boss, known to everyone as Old Man Sullivan, died. His only child, the power-hungry Aaron Sullivan Jr., was in charge now. Will knew him as a loudmouthed jock who had been a few years ahead of him in high school. Aaron was the kind of guy who liked to shove people around and flaunt his money and connections. Everyone had expected him to go to some rich college far away. They had expected Will to stay behind and work at the mill. Funny how things turn out.

It was a local legend that the Sullivans had a fortune in gold and the old grudges that went along with it. Aaron could have pulled up stakes and gone wherever he wanted. But when Old Man Sullivan died, much of the SulCorp gold went missing. The mystery had never been solved. Aaron became as stuck as any other Hope resident.

Now Will was back in the place he had sworn never to return to, and all because his own dad was dead.

"Sulfur," Will whispered and then turned away.

Chapter Three

Will stood outside the old Trainstop apartment building. It sat right beside the old railroad tracks that cut a dead end into the town. The building and tracks were next to the massive sulfur mill and the bordering river and forest.

A car pulled up, kicking gravel as it came to a sudden halt. It was an ancient Oldsmobile, a real boat of a car, but the V8 engine purred.

Will recognized it right away. It was the kind of car a cop likes to drive, and not just any cop. It belonged to his dad's old partner, Detective Jim Rivers.

The driver's door swung out on its hinges with a creaking noise. A tall man in his sixties unfolded himself from behind the wheel.

Rivers always seemed like he was wearing someone else's clothes. They were bland and neutral-colored. The pants were too short. He had the look of someone pretending to be a person. Not exactly the kind of cop you see on TV.

"How did you know I was here?" Will asked, but of course it was a stupid question. Rivers knew everything that went on in Hope.

The older man lit a smoke and took a deep drag. "You're kidding, right?" His face softened and grew more serious as he added, "Sorry about the old man, kid."

Will nodded. "Was he drunk again?"

Rivers nodded. "You know your dad. What do you think?"

Will shrugged.

"It's been a long time, kid," said Rivers. "I didn't know where you went. Your dad didn't say."

"Wouldn't say," said Will.

"Yeah, makes sense," said Rivers, taking another drag. "What with all the gold that went missing." Smoke seeped out of his mouth as he smiled. "And you being suspect number one."

"You know that I didn't take that gold," Will said through gritted teeth.

"Do I?" asked Rivers. He puffed on the smoke again, burning it down almost to the filter. "Whether I do or not, it seems like an awful lot of people around here think you did. And then you disappeared."

Will shrugged. "I had to get away. Too much happened and…" He trailed off.

"Some people think the past is in the past," said Rivers. "But you and I both know that's a load of shit."

"Look," said Will. "I'm here to deal with my dad. I don't want trouble, and I don't want to bring up old shit."

"Whoa," said Rivers. "Hold on, kid. I'm not saying anything. I'm not here to give you a hard time. I know you're going through it. Your dad… hell, Bill was my friend for a long time. He'd want to know I was looking out for you."

Rivers stubbed out his smoke with his boot. "There's a lot of people around here who would love to get their mitts on you." He pointed across the street at the SulCorp sign. "And Sullivan's one of them. You best believe young Aaron knows you're here."

"He'd be counting on it," said Will.

"Aaron's running things now," said Rivers. "All that shady stuff Old Man Sullivan was into has only ramped up. Aaron is looser with the law than his old man was. And now with your dad... It has happened before, you know? Not the first dead body I've pulled from the sulfur. Hope it's the last."

"So you're saying my dad turning up in a pile of sulfur wasn't such an accident," said Will.

Rivers shook his head. "Not an accident at all. But not a murder either."

"Huh?"

"My theory is he'd had enough," said Rivers. "Wanted to end it. He was in bad shape, Will."

"What are you saying?" Will asked.

Rivers sighed. "He took his own life, Will. I know you don't want to hear it."

"I don't," said Will. "Because it's bullshit."

Rivers held up his hands. "It's the truth."

"No," said Will. "But I promise you that I will find out the real truth. You know Sullivan had to be involved."

"Careful, kid," Rivers said. "What's your plan? You're just gonna stroll back to town, no friends, all alone, and take on the guy who hates your guts?"

Will shook his head. "I'm not alone," he said. "I've got you, Uncle Jim."

Rivers grinned. "Tell you what. You keep your nose clean while you're here, and I'll make sure no one tries to get a piece of you. But you have to promise me something."

"What?" Will asked.

"You'll stay away from Eve Hart."

Will swallowed hard, his pulse quickening at the mention of her name. "I can't do that."

"Listen," said Rivers. "That girl has her head all twisted around. Best to take care of business and then get the hell outta here."

Will said nothing.

"You need a place to stay?"

"No." Will shook his head. "I got it covered."

"Then I guess I'll see you tomorrow afternoon," said Rivers. "Say, three o'clock?"

"For what?" asked Will.

"The hospital," said Rivers. "The morgue. You'll need to sign off. If you want to bury your dad. You are eighteen now, right? You had a birthday?"

Will nodded, unable to say anything at the moment.

"If it's too hard, you can leave the official stuff to me," said Rivers.

"No," said Will. "But I thought there would be more of an investigation."

Rivers shook his head. "What's there to investigate? The bad medicine finally caught up with Bill. No use in poking around after a suicide. It only prolongs the pain."

Will let that sink in. "I'll be there," he said. "I need to see him."

"Good," said Rivers. "Be careful, kid. And, uh,

if you find anything interesting in that pigsty apartment of his, let me know."

"Like what?" Will asked. "Are you looking for something?"

Rivers smiled, but it didn't reach his eyes. "Old habits, I guess," he said. "I'm always looking." With that he climbed back into his car and drove away.

Will watched the taillights fade into the darkness.

———

Will looked around at the outdated lobby of the Trainstop. The shag carpet was a swirl of stains and patterns. There was a cigarette machine next to the stairwell.

It was a haunted place, full of memories. He remembered the first time he met Eve. It was here, in this lobby.

Will had been sitting on the bottom step of the stairwell, reading a history textbook. From the floor above had come shouting, then the slamming of a door, then the sound of someone running down the stairs.

He remembered how Eve had come barreling toward him, how she'd tripped on the last step and fallen face down on the floor in front of him. He'd tried to help her up, but she wouldn't let him. She'd had a bloody nose.

He'd asked if she was okay, knowing it was a stupid question. She wasn't okay, not a girl like her. There were old, fading yellow bruises on her cheek and arms. But when she'd wiped the blood away, she seemed unfazed.

The first thing she'd done was ask him for money. He hadn't had any, but if he had, he would have given her every cent. Before long he'd found himself babbling about his entire life, even his mom's death. That had seemed to soften her, and she'd told him she'd be his best friend if he would buy her some smokes.

"What's in it for me?" he'd asked.

Her answer rang in his mind. *My undying love.*

Will walked up the steps toward the second floor and pushed open the heavy fire door at the top. He stepped into the second-floor hallway and walked over to a dingy door numbered 2B. He took a key from his pocket, one he hadn't used in two years. He slid it into the knob and turned the lock.

The small apartment overflowed with clutter. Photos, newspapers and empty dishes covered the floor. His dad's life surrounded Will. Despite the grunge, the place had a sense of warmth. Will settled into the cozy armchair in front of the TV. He relaxed back into the knitted purple blanket that covered it.

A few minutes later Will rummaged through his dad's closet and pulled up a floorboard underneath the worn carpet. He pulled out a shoebox. Inside was a 9mm handgun. He picked up the gun, released the clip, checked it and then snapped it back inside. He placed it in the waistband of his jeans, at the small of his back. He might need it. Rivers' warning had put the fear into him again.

A pair of handcuffs glinted in the box. Will picked them up and turned them over in his hands. He paused when he saw something else in there. His father's police badge. He picked it up with shaking hands.

"I'm sorry," he whispered. Will placed the cuffs and badge in his bag. He looked at the time on his phone: 1:03 a.m. He looked over at the unmade bed and then turned to go. He couldn't stay there, surrounded by his dad's things, and it wasn't safe.

He pulled out his phone and sent a message.

I'm here, Aunt Justine. I'm safe.

Going to stay at a motel. Saw Uncle Jim.

Going to see Dad tomorrow.

After a moment the reply came.

And Eve?

Will you see her?

Will didn't answer. He grabbed his bag and left. Would he see Eve? If he could have his way, he'd be with her right now. He'd find her and hold her and never leave her.

Only trouble was, he didn't know if she felt the same way.

Chapter Four

The Budget Motel was right on the highway on the outskirts of town. The mountains loomed overhead.

Will stood at the counter and smacked the desk bell. Instead of a loud ding, all that came out was a hollow clink.

There was a small television hanging in an

overhead corner. It was showing the weather forecast. Rain.

Will smirked to himself and muttered, "What else is new?"

A toilet flushed, and a side door opened off the lobby. It was the desk clerk, a guy in his early twenties with long, straight hair pulled back in a ponytail. He was carrying a newspaper.

"Hey, sorry about that, man," he said to Will. "Duty called, you know? Need a room?"

Will nodded. "Yeah. Got one?"

"That's all I got, man. Not much tourism around here anymore. Whole town's gone to shit. Or sulfur, I should say. Smells the same." The clerk chuckled and then paused when he reached the counter. He stared at Will for a long beat.

"Holy shit," he said finally. "You came back."

Will shifted from foot to foot. "Do we know each other?"

"Dude. You don't remember all those parties at Toby's place? You and your little friends would hang around hoping we'd take pity on you and give you some beers."

"Oh." Will paused, finally placing the guy. "Ryan, right?"

"Yeah, dude," said Ryan. "Man, I never thought I'd see you back here. Not after everything."

"That makes two of us," said Will.

On the television, a news story came on. The banner across the bottom of the screen identified the young reporter as Nigel Beatty. He was standing outside the sulfur mill.

Will stiffened.

"It seems the disgraced ex-cop died of an alleged suicide late last night," said the reporter.

Ryan looked up and shook his head at the television. "Would you look at this guy?" he said. "Nigel acts like he owns the town, and he only got the job because the other reporter retired. You know he's editor at the paper too? Seems like yesterday he was delivering the newspaper here. Now I gotta read his bullshit in the paper, on his little website, and I gotta watch him on TV every day. Far cry from the little freak he used to be in high school, hey?"

Will stared at the television, seething. "Yeah," he said.

Ryan studied Will's face. "Hey, man. I didn't mean to bring up old shit."

"Don't worry about it," Will muttered.

Ryan reached behind him and grabbed a key off the hanging board.

"It's $48.50 a night," said Ryan. "But first night's on the house if you stay the week. I'm supposed to get a credit card from you, and you're supposed to be of age, but I guess you're on your own now, huh?"

Will stared at him.

Ryan smirked and slid the key over to Will. "You're good for it, right? I mean, you gotta still have some of that gold left."

Will said nothing as he pulled crumpled bills from his back pocket. He placed them on the counter, picked up the key and headed toward the door. "There was never any gold," he said over his shoulder. "And I'm not staying that long."

A photo of a younger Will flashed on the screen. Nigel Beatty continued his report, his voice following Will out the door. "Now, many wonder if Hope's most infamous resident will return. Is the 'hero' man enough to come back? And what about the SulCorp fortune? Will anyone find the mysterious gold?"

———

Inside room 7 at the Budget Motel, Will slept in spurts between nightmares.

A winch pulls the bloated, blue-faced corpse from deep within a sulfur pile and dangles it by its boots. Yellow powder lands on Will's upturned face. Will flinches as the dust falls into his eyes. He brushes it away. He looks down and notices yellow smudges covering his coat and the palms of his hands.

The corpse wears a security uniform and has a name tag that reads Bill.

"Dad," whispers Will. "It finally caught up with you…"

Will woke on the stained bedspread covering one of the ancient twin beds in the room. He had sweated through his undershirt. He read the clock: 1:39 p.m. He stood up, stretched his stiff body and opened the curtains. An overcast afternoon. He threw on some jeans and a T-shirt, grabbed his jacket and headed out the door.

Will bought a tiny cup of inky coffee from a dispenser and then bought a chocolate bar from the vending machine. It would have to do. He looked back at the diner, wishing it was still open for breakfast.

As he walked back toward his room, he passed a newspaper stand. The headline caught his eye. *HOPE'S "HERO" HOME.*

"Great," he said, grabbing a copy.

There was a photo of Will, the same one used on the TV last night, alongside a photo of Eve. Will scanned the cover story. Words popped out from the text. *Dead sulfur tycoon, missing girl, missing gold.*

Will clenched the paper in his hands. He closed his eyes for a moment and then opened them again. The story's byline read *Nigel Beatty, Editor.* A small black-and-white photo of Nigel smirked up at him.

"That son of a bitch," Will muttered. He threw the paper in the trash and walked across the parking lot to the highway. A police car rolled down the road. Will kept his eyes on the ground.

Chapter Five

Will entered a long hallway at the Hope hospital and took a deep breath.

Detective Rivers stood leaning against a set of heavy green metal double doors. He puffed on a cigarette despite the No Smoking sign posted on the wall right beside him. When he saw Will coming, he took a deep drag and then snuffed the butt out on the linoleum with his heel.

"Hey, kid," said Rivers. "You settling back in okay? Seeing old friends yet?"

Will ignored his questions and eyed the doors.

"He's in there? My dad?" Will asked.

Rivers nodded. "Want me to come in with you?"

Will shook his head. "No. I want to get this over with."

Rivers opened the door for him and stepped aside.

Inside, a man in a lab coat waited beside a body on a gurney covered by a white sheet. He held out a gloved hand to Will as he approached and then pulled off the glove to shake hands.

"Good to see you home again, Will," he said.

Will shook his hand. "Hi," he said, and then remembered the man as one of his dad's old friends. "Dave, right?"

He nodded. "I'll make this as quick as I can," said Dave. "You ready?" He pulled back the sheet.

Will looked down. For a long moment he felt nothing. He didn't blink. He didn't breathe. He didn't cry. Even his heart didn't seem to beat.

That was his dad on the table. He looked the same as he had a couple of years earlier, but a little smaller, as if dying had made him shrink. A pang of guilt ripped through Will.

"Is this your father, William Homer?" asked Dave.

Will swallowed hard. "Yes," he said.

Dave replaced the sheet and pulled out a clipboard. "Sign here," he said.

Will signed with a trembling hand and then dropped the pen. He ran his hands through his hair and clasped them behind his neck. He spoke in a strangled voice. "What will it say in your report?" he asked. "The cause of death? Will it be a suicide?"

"That is not certain," said Dave. "I know what killed him, but I'm not sure if it was intentional," said Dave.

Will stared at him. "Tell me what you found. Please."

Dave hesitated. "Look, things aren't what they seem around here, and it won't do any good at this point."

"I'm not the same kid I used to be," said Will.

Dave sighed. "It wasn't suffocation in the sulfur that killed your father, but it was the sulfur at the same time."

"I don't follow," Will said.

"Cleanup crews found a flask in the sulfur long after police had cleared the body. The flask had his initials on it. You know the one?"

Will nodded. "I know the one."

"And there wasn't only alcohol in it," said Dave. "There was something else mixed in."

"What?" asked Will.

Dave looked at Will as if he knew the next words he said would change everything.

"What was in it?" Will prodded.

Dave's face grew tight. "It's a new drug the kids are taking around here," he said. "They call it Hell's Gate. Powerful narcotic." Dave paused. "It's a sulfur-based compound," he continued. "There was enough in there to poison him."

There was a long pause as the two stared at each other. Will felt like he was about to throw up, but he fought it off.

"Sulfur. Of course it would be sulfur," he said. "But wouldn't my dad have known?"

"Not with how drunk he'd been getting," said Dave. "You know, Bill and I kept in touch. I went to see him once a week. To check in, you know. He missed you. But he was proud. And," he added, "he was killing himself with booze."

Will nodded.

"Listen," said Dave. "I have no allegiance to the cops in this town. Not after the way they did your dad dirty, and the awful stuff from before. I'm close to retiring. My job is to see the bodies through the door, but this one…I can't let go. Bill was a real friend. And you deserve to know that this business about his death being a suicide is wrong. Call it laziness, sloppy work, whatever. I couldn't stand you not knowing."

"Thank you, Dave."

"If there's anything I can do…your dad, well, he was one of the good ones."

Will slipped out the door past Rivers. Several more spent cigarette butts were on the floor.

"Hey," Rivers said, starting to follow him. "What did the doc say? Will? Will!"

Will ignored him and strode out the exit as fast as he could.

Chapter Six

The Armory pub was in the center of town. It was a seedy little place built of bricks that were now crumbling. Its blue neon lights flickered and buzzed like bug zappers. They reflected off the puddles that lined the sidewalk outside.

Will huddled in the small space in front of the heavy wooden door. The ever-present mist of rain had turned into a downpour. He wasn't worried about getting in or getting served. For one, he didn't drink, and two, no one asked for ID in this town. He didn't want to go in because it felt like rejoining a world he'd worked so hard to leave behind.

The door opened and a drunk stumbled through. The sounds of bar music, clinking glasses and loud conversation spilled out.

Will checked his watch and then slipped inside. He found a seat away from the rowdy crowd, at a corner table by himself. He put his back to the wall and fixed his eyes on the door.

A guy holding two beers veered in front of his table and stopped to stare at him.

"Fuck," muttered Will. "Hey, Toby," he said a bit louder. There was no point in pretending he didn't recognize him. Toby would sit down anyway. He slid in next to Will without sloshing a drop of beer, drained one pint and then started in on the other.

Toby was one of those legendary guys from high school—there were always a million stories about him. He had no parents and had his own house outside of town. He'd always had the best weed and threw parties that people remembered years later. Toby always drank more than everyone else but never seemed drunk.

He should have been a mess, but Will remembered him as a solid guy. He wasn't exactly not happy to see Toby so much as not prepared. Toby had been a friend once upon a time, and now he sat looking at Will with one eyebrow raised in his sharp, pointy face. It was a face that could cut glass.

"Well, look here," said Toby. "If it isn't the hero himself. How you doin', man? And why the hell did you come back to this shithole?"

Will shrugged. "Couldn't stay away from you, I guess," he said.

"I always knew you were in love with me," said Toby. He smiled wide, and Will couldn't help but smile back.

"I heard about your dad," said Toby, growing more serious—or as serious as he was capable of being. "Shit, that's a raw deal. Burying your dad...that's rough."

No one understood that better than Toby.

"Well, it's good to see you, at least," said Will.

"The news surprised me," said Toby. "But I guess the sulfur gets us all, in time."

"Don't tell me they got you working there now," said Will.

"Fuck no," said Toby. "But the way the shit runs, I could be."

"What do you mean?" asked Will.

Toby ignored him and turned toward the barkeep, a big old Swede named Sam with a neck wider than Will's thigh. Sam looked like he'd be more at home swinging a sword on an ancient battlefield than pouring drinks.

"Hey, Sam!" Toby called. "Baby! Give my buddy a beer, eh?"

"Sure, honey," said Sam. He winked, poured a pint and placed it on the counter.

Toby hurried over to collect it, planting a kiss on Sam in the process. He brought the drink back to the table and set it down, a satisfied smile on his face.

"Wait, so you and Sam...?" Will asked. "I always thought you had a thing for Nigel in high school."

Toby sputtered on his beer as he laughed. "Um, no. Nigel Beatty was most definitely not my type back in high school, and he sure as hell isn't now. God, have you seen his awful blog? Who does he think he is?"

"Unfortunately I have," said Will.

"What are the odds?" Toby carried on, gazing over at Sam. "In this shitty town? I can't believe I managed to snag the only bear not taken. And he's a hot Viking. Score for me."

Will grinned. "Cheers to that."

"Cheers, buddy," said Toby, clinking his glass against Will's.

But Will didn't drink. He left the glass sitting there untouched.

"So why are you here?" Toby asked.

"I'm not," he said.

"I mean, why are you actually here?" Toby asked again. "Is it because of the Sullivan gold? Is it…Eve?" That sharp eyebrow went up again. Toby was no fool.

Will shifted. "It might be better if I don't see her."

Toby laughed. "Okay. Well, if you don't want to see her, you shouldn't hang around here much.

I'm not saying she works here, her being underage and all, but I'm not *not* saying that." He glanced around. "I don't see her. She must be late again."

"That's good," said Will. He had to resist asking Toby everything he knew about Eve. He wanted to see her more than anything in the world, but for her own good he needed to stay away.

"Tell me that when she finds out you're here," said Toby with a smirk. "We'll see how long you can resist her."

"I told you," Will said with a sigh. "I'm not here."

"Well, while you're *not* here, we have some partying to do. Like old times." Toby raised his glass and drained it.

"Sure," said Will. "You could hook me up with something."

"Yeah? What's your poison?" Toby asked.

Will tensed at the mention of poison. "I need information," he said. "What do you know about Hell's Gate?"

Toby stared at Will. "Did you know I'd be here tonight? Did you come here for me?"

"Aren't you always here?" Will asked, unfazed.

The two stared at each other, and then Toby started laughing.

"Yeah, well, I guess I am. Especially now that my bae works here. Tell you what. You give me a call later, and we'll hang, okay? We can talk about recreational drugs. My number is the same. Always the same. You still got it?" Toby stood up to leave.

"Yeah, I got it. I'll see you," said Will.

"Unless he sees you first," said Toby under his breath.

Will leaned forward. "What was that?" he asked.

Toby walked away but shot Will a worried glance and nodded to the door.

Will got up to follow Toby. They walked out the door. Toby shook Will's hand and slipped him a piece of paper before he walked away. Will pocketed it without reacting and looked around. There was no one on the street, but he felt like he was being watched all the same.

The rain came down harder, and Will retreated into the broken phone booth outside the pub. There was no receiver anymore. Graffiti covered the booth. He took out his phone and dialed a number. It went to voice mail. There was no name. An electronic voice said to leave a message.

"Hi, Aunt Justine," said Will when he heard the beep. "It's me." He paused. "I'm not sure yet when I'll be back. Things are more complicated than I thought." He fiddled with the paper Toby had given him. "But I have a way of getting some answers." He ended the call without saying goodbye. He unfolded the paper and on it were two words:

He's watching.

Will stepped out of the booth and jumped at the sight of a dark-haired girl. Their eyes locked. Will's blue eyes and her big brown ones.

"Eve," he said, breathless.

She was wearing a very short skirt and high-heeled boots, though her top had a high neck and long sleeves. She was carrying a tray of drinks. Rain collected in the glasses, mingling with the alcohol.

Eve stared at Will. Then she hurled the tray, glasses and all, right at his head.

Will ducked. The glass shattered against the phone booth, shards and rainwater and booze spraying him.

"You're going to ruin everything!" she yelled.

"I…" Will started. But he didn't know what to say.

Eve spun on her heel and ran in the opposite direction down the street, her long black hair trailing behind.

Will stared after her.

A black BMW, slick with rain, rolled by. The hood ornament was a glinting chrome SulCorp logo.

The rear passenger-side window lowered enough to show a man's dark eyes looking out at Will. Heavy blue cigar smoke puffed from the window.

He took a step toward it, and the BMW sped off.

"Fuck this town," said Will.

Chapter Seven

Back at his father's apartment, Will sat on the sagging couch and held his father's badge in his hands. He set it down and picked up his dad's gun, latching and unlatching the safety over and over again.

Will's packed duffel bag rested at his feet, and an unopened bottle of cheap scotch sat on the coffee table in front of him. Choices, he thought. Stay or go. Drink or don't drink. Was he all the way in or all the way out? And did he have the guts to do what he needed to?

Finally he unclipped the gun and stuck it in his bag before pulling up Aunt Justine on his phone:

Saw old friends, but this town is poison. I won't be coming home yet. Have to stay and sort some things out.

As soon as he had sent the text, he deleted it from his phone. He leaned back and stared at the bottle of scotch. There was a little lamp next to him on the side table. He flicked it off, then on, then off again, flashing the messy room from light to darkness.

Memories of Eve, of her voice and her body, echoed in his mind. He imagined her coming out of the darkness. Her mouth on his. How she tasted.

He shook his head. This place was getting to him. He needed some peace and quiet to think things through, and he sure as hell would not be able to do that in this apartment. It felt too much like his dad. Too many memories making noise in his head.

He grabbed his duffel bag, got up, and walked to the door. When he opened it, Detective Rivers was on the other side, about to knock.

"We got a problem, kid," he said.

Will dropped his duffel bag. "What did you find?"

"More questions," said Rivers. "Story of my life. Nothing can ever rest—even your poor father."

He strode in past Will, his large frame seeming to take up all the space in the small room, and sat down.

Will sat across from him as Rivers looked around the room.

"Your old man never cleaned up, did he?" asked Rivers.

"He liked to hold on to stuff," said Will. "Or at least try to."

"He let you go," Rivers pointed out.

"He had to," said Will.

"It ain't easy being on the job so long," said Rivers. "It gets to be all you understand. It's like being in a prison, only we're supposed to be the good guys. But you get older, like me and your dad, and you realize there's no such thing as good guys and bad guys. There's what needs doing and there's being strong enough to do it."

Will stared at him. Rivers had never looked so old or so tired before. "There's still right and wrong," said Will.

"And you know all about that, huh?" asked Rivers. "Tell me, kid, was it wrong of you to leave town the way you did? Leave your dad to clean up the mess? Leave your girl and your friends behind? You left me here trying to close the loop on Old Man Sullivan's crimes. And the gold—"

"Tell me what you found," Will interrupted.

"I talked to Dave," said Rivers. "From the morgue."

Will straightened up. "What did he tell you?"

"Your dad didn't die by suicide," he said. "Someone killed him."

Will said nothing.

"This changes everything," said Rivers. "It means an investigation. I thought it was all taken care of. Now I have to reopen the books."

"How was he killed?" Will asked.

Rivers shook his head. "Unclear. Dave said he'd get back to me on all that." Rivers lit a cigarette and blew out a long plume of smoke.

Will took all this in. Dave hadn't told Rivers about the poisoning. There had to be a reason for that.

"If anyone can figure it out, I'm sure it's you," said Will.

Rivers shook his head. "If I had some help."

"What kind?" Will asked.

"If I could figure out what Bill was hiding, I could find out who killed him," said Rivers.

"Hiding?" Will asked.

Rivers pulled out a small black notebook with a flip top, the kind used by cops. It had the initials *WH* on it.

His dad's notebook.

"Where did you get that?" Will asked.

"I got it off his body," said Rivers. "At the crime scene."

"What's in it?" Will asked.

"He took notes on everything," said Rivers. "Old cop habits die hard."

"I want it," said Will.

Rivers nodded. "Sure thing. But I want you to see this entry first."

He opened the notebook and passed it to Will. In writing that became shakier and shakier, Will's dad had written mysterious notes.

10:15 p.m. He's following me.

Must keep it hidden.

Buried treasure stays buried.

"What does this mean?" Will asked. His heart began to pound in his chest.

Rivers stared at Will, his eyes seeming to bore right through him. "I was hoping you could tell me."

"I-I don't know," Will said.

"You see," said Rivers, "I thought your dad was paranoid when I read this. Case of the DTs, you know? But he was onto something." He paused and stubbed out his cigarette in an empty beer bottle. "And it had something to do with you."

"Me?" asked Will.

Rivers nodded. He leaned forward in his chair, and Will tried not to squirm under his gaze. How many criminals had Rivers interrogated in his career? How many people had felt this weird, burning pressure when he questioned them?

"Not only that, but it involves your sweetheart, Eve. And the Sullivan gold."

Will shook his head. "No. No way."

Rivers smirked. "Hell, I figured that you'd made off with a fortune all those years ago, but your dad always insisted you hadn't. Your old man was a lot of things, but he wasn't a liar. So what happened to it?"

"I don't know anything about the gold."

"You were there," said Rivers. "At the crime scene when Old Man Sullivan died. The only other person there was Eve," said Rivers.

"You're forgetting about several of Hope's finest cops," said Will. "Anyone could have taken it. Even you!"

Rivers lit another cigarette. "Ah, but you were the only one who left town."

Will sighed and sat back in his chair.

"Now, we all know what a creep Old Man Sullivan was," said Rivers. "No one could blame you for what happened. You saved that girl. And let's say you didn't take the gold. But you know where it is. Or your dad did. And if we can find it, then we can find his killer. I have a pretty good idea who it was."

"Who?" Will asked.

Rivers took a drag. "The new Mr. Sulfur, of course."

"Aaron," said Will. "That's who you've got your money on?"

Rivers blew out a puff of smoke. "That snake is just like his old man. I wouldn't put it past him to have done this out of spite."

Will considered this. "To hurt me."

Rivers nodded. "Hell, I even got a call from him. He wants a meeting."

There was a long pause as the two looked at each other.

"He knows you're here," said Rivers. "He's always watching."

Will shuddered, remembering Toby's note. "When do we do this?" he asked.

"Tomorrow night. We want to get a read on him so we know how to nail him for this."

Will got up and walked across the room. He looked at his duffel bag, then at the door, then at Rivers. "What do I do here?" he asked. "What do I choose?"

"Choose?" Rivers shook his head. "You can leave. Forget all this and try to live your life. But—"

"But," Will finished for him, "you know I can't do that."

Rivers shrugged. "Then why ask?"

"Fine," said Will. "Pick me up tomorrow night. Let's get this over with."

Chapter Eight

The next afternoon Will stood in the doorway of the Armory. He was dripping wet from the rain.

He watched as Eve worked the room, serving drinks to everyone. She floated through the bar as if it were a grand ballroom. She twirled on her high heels, a kind of dark ballerina tuned into her own music.

He watched her feet in her red shoes.

Eve spun and placed a glass brimming with beer on a table. She smiled a studied smile, but when her back turned the smile fell.

She looked up and saw Will. Her eyes connected with his.

They stood still for a long beat, looking into each other across the bar.

All was silent for them in that moment, though the action of the bar was in full swing. People danced, played pool, argued with each other and spilled drinks. But Eve and Will existed only for each other. She walked toward him as if in slow motion.

"I need your help," said Will as she got closer.

"I know," she said.

"It's weird," he said. "History is repeating itself."

Their eyes locked, the attraction unmistakable.

———

They drank coffee at a plastic table on the sidewalk outside Bobby's Diner along the highway.

The wind picked up, and Eve shivered against it. The cars made a whooshing sound as they passed, like waves crashing on a beach.

"I like watching traffic," said Eve. "All those people. Their lives going by. Everyone's leaving and I'm going nowhere."

Will stared at her. "Why did you throw those drinks at me?" he asked.

Her smile grew. "I was angry," she said.

"Yeah," said Will. "I had your anger all over me."

"Well, it looked good on you." Her smile disappeared. "I thought you'd write or something."

"I couldn't," said Will. "It was too risky. I needed to stay gone. Until I was ready to come back."

"You're ready now?"

He shook his head. "No choice."

"Do you know what it was like not knowing if I'd see you again?" she asked. "Having to trust that I was still on your mind? I've been frozen since you left."

Will reached over and dragged her chair closer to his. "I'm sorry I made you wait so long."

———

Back at Will's motel, they had sex on the bed in the bright room. Eve was on top of Will and was still wearing most of her clothes. She'd only taken off her underwear. Will was shirtless, and Eve clutched at his chest, her eyes closed tight. Will was wearing only his pushed-down jeans and his boots. There'd been no time to take it slow. How could they? They clutched at each other, desperate. Will stared up at her, watching her as she tensed up and then fell back against his chest.

He traced his fingers across her shoulders. The edge of a tattoo peeked from under her collar. She shivered.

He smoothed her shirt back in place. "You okay?"

She sighed. "Sometimes it feels like I'm still in that cement room," she whispered. "Tied up in the dark."

"You're free," he said.

She climbed off him and curled up next to him.

"Eve," Will said. "I'm sorry. I wish I had gotten there sooner."

"It wouldn't have mattered," she said. "Girl like me, town like this—there's always someone waiting for their turn."

She rested her head on his chest, and he tightened his arms around her. She continued talking, her voice haunted. "I knew he was dead. All that blood…" She shuddered.

"Maybe we shouldn't do this," Will said. "We could just leave. Together."

Eve closed her eyes as Will stroked her hair.

"Too late," she said. She opened her eyes and looked up at him. "We have to get through the next steps."

He sighed. "Here. I want you to have something."

"What?"

He reached over and pulled his father's badge from his bag. He handed it to her.

"Why are you giving this to me?" she asked.

"It's the one thing I have that matters. And if something happens to me…"

"Stop it," she said, a tremor in her voice.

"I need you to hide it," he said. "The way only you can."

She nodded and held the badge.

Will got up, dressed and retrieved his father's gun from under his pillow.

"Where are you going?" she asked.

"Meeting someone. I came back here to do something, and I'm going to get it done. I need some more proof."

"What more could you need?" she asked.

"It's okay. I'll be back soon. Wait?"

"For a while," she said.

He turned off the light and moved to open the door.

Eve sat up, panic on her face. "Will! The light!"

He stopped, backed up and reached for the light switch. He turned it on and went out the door.

Chapter Nine

Rivers pulled up to SulCorp's main gate. The mill grounds were off the highway, with a river on one side and railroad tracks on the other. From up above on the hillside road, the site looked like a lopsided heart.

"Ready?" asked Rivers.

"One second," said Will.

Will stared out at the mill. He heard machinery churning, railcars crashing and metal scraping. Huge piles of sulfur reached skyward. Their pyramid shapes gleamed yellow in the night. Rotating rakes smoothed their sloping sides. Small buckets on a loop scooped the loose powder at the bottom and brought it back up to the top.

Conveyor lines snaked in between them like arteries feeding blood to and from a heart. They carried the gleaming dust between stacks and buildings to small railcars with *SulTrain* painted on the sides. The cars shuttled back and forth, delivering sulfur to waiting boats, larger railcars or trucks for shipment.

"Now or never, kid," Rivers said.

Will shoved open his door and got out.

Just past the archway, at the main entrance door, Rivers pressed the intercom button.

A voice deep and raspy, like a smoker's, came through the dingy speaker box. "Proceed," it said.

A buzz sounded, and the heavy metal door swung open. Rivers stepped forward, but Will stopped.

"What is it, kid?" Rivers asked.

Will shivered. "I can't help the memories. Being here. It makes me feel the same way I did that night."

"I get it," said Rivers. "Hard to forget that kind of thing. I know I'll never forget seeing you covered in someone else's blood. Can't imagine how your dad felt."

Will nodded. "I was so worried for him when he told me to go, to cut and run and not look back. I don't know if I would have done the same thing in his situation."

Rivers took a deep drag off his smoke. "Sure you would have," he said. "You would have wanted your kid to get out of this place too. Especially after something like that. This is Hope, Will. Nothing good happens here."

Will sighed. "I didn't realize it would cost him his job. The last time I saw him, I was leaving on a bus. I was looking back at him through the rear window. He was standing under a streetlight." Will fought back tears. "I kept watching as he got smaller and smaller." Will shook his head as if clearing the painful memory.

"No use dwelling on that," Rivers said. "We have to take care of this now."

They walked forward into the mill, past piles of machine parts and supplies. They reached a large sulfur pile in the center of the works yard.

Rivers lit another cigarette.

"Is this where my dad died?" Will asked.

"Yeah. Buried halfway."

Will was silent as he walked closer to the pile.

The yellow was the brightest thing in the darkness. He looked at Rivers. The sulfur cast such an intense glow that Rivers seemed to be lit by a sickly spotlight.

A loud clang made Will jump. A metal office door had swung open on the building nearby. It was their invitation to enter.

Once inside the office, they stood in a cloud of blue cigar smoke. Factory soot and grease was on every surface.

A tall, thin young man with black hair stepped from a darkened corner. Aaron Sullivan Jr., heir to the SulCorp throne, puffed a fine cigar. He ran his buffed nails on the soft silk of his expensive suit. He stroked himself like a giant cat. It was clear he didn't spend much time in the grimy office, and he definitely didn't get his hands dirty. He was a few years older than Will, and he still had the same air of superiority he'd had back when they were kids.

Aaron nodded at them. He looked at Will, a sly smile playing at the corner of his mouth. "So," he said. "You came."

"You remember—" Rivers began.

"Little Willy Junior," said Aaron, cutting him off. He stared at Will with his black eyes. "My condolences," he said. "Imagine all this time gone by, wondering if you'd ever come back. And all it took was one old drunk guy to off himself."

Will winced, and Aaron smirked.

"He was a good man," said Will.

Aaron turned to Rivers. "It's funny how things change depending on your perspective, isn't it, Detective?"

Rivers cocked his head to the side. He seemed uneasy with the intensity radiating through the room. "Enough with the pleasantries," he said. "You called us here, Aaron. What do you want?"

Aaron blew smoke at them. "To see the person responsible for all this." He looked at Will and winked.

"Oh, and by the way, Detective," he said, "from now on, if you want to sniff around my mill, you're going to need a warrant. It's one thing to invite you here so I can see my old pal Will. It's another to find out you've been trespassing. Snooping around."

Will shot Rivers a questioning look.

Rivers ignored Aaron's accusation and stepped forward. His face took on a blank look—the look Will recognized as the detective's interrogation face. "Why would I need a warrant?" Rivers asked. "Do you have something to hide?"

Aaron let loose a rasping laugh. "That's a good one, Jimbo. You have no idea how funny that is."

"Answer the question."

"We all have something to hide," Aaron said. "Don't we?" He looked at Will. "And some of us are desperate to find things."

"What does that mean?" asked Rivers.

Will spoke up. "Look, I came to settle my father's affairs. Not to get involved in old shit."

Aaron smiled. "Ah, well. No avoiding that, I'm afraid." He stubbed out his cigar. "Do me a favor.

When you put your father in the ground, think of me, and you'll know how I felt."

Will bristled. "Watch what you say."

Aaron laughed. "We all know what brought us here. My father is dead and his fortune lost. And you"—he pointed at Will—"are the connection."

"I don't have that gold," said Will through gritted teeth.

"Oh, I know," said Aaron. "And Jim knows it too, don't you?"

Rivers glared at him.

"What do you mean?" Will asked.

"It's hidden away," said Rivers. "That's as much as we know."

"My father always said no one would find the gold," said Aaron. "And no one has."

"So you mean all this time people have accused me of taking it, you both knew I didn't?" Will's voice shook.

Rivers turned to him. "We couldn't let that information get out. It was better for people to think it was gone. No use having a lot of lowlifes searching for a stash of hidden gold bars. It would be the Wild West around here."

"Sure," said Aaron. "That's the reason."

"And you have no idea where it is?" asked Will.

Aaron shrugged. "Can't find the map."

"M-map?" Will stammered. "Who said anything about a map?"

"It was something your dad said before he turned up in the sulfur," said Rivers, nodding at Will. "He thought there was a map. Only…we can't find it."

Will took a step back. "So you've been keeping a lot from me, huh?"

"Will, look—"

Aaron cut Rivers off. "Detective, you'd better get your friend out of here before this goes too far."

"Hey, I'm not done talking to you," said Will.

"But I'm done talking to you," said Aaron.

"Come on, kid." Rivers took Will by the shoulder and steered him out of the room.

As they left, Will looked back. Aaron stared after them. The smile had fallen from his face. A weary sadness had taken over.

Will turned away. He knew that look well.

Chapter Ten

Rivers dropped Will off at the motel. He warned him again to stay away from Eve. Little did he know that she was sleeping inside Will's room.

Will slipped in and curled up next to Eve on the bed, folding his frame around her. She roused a bit and wiggled a little closer to him. Their limbs tangled. Will couldn't get enough of her. The way her soft skin felt under his hands, what it felt like to be so connected to her.

Soon she was pushing her underwear down, and he was kissing the inside of her thighs. This was all he ever wanted. To make her feel good. And he would ask for nothing in return. He'd dreamed about this. Worshipping her. She cried out his name.

After, when she had gone back to sleep, Will breathed in the smell of her. It was like the mineral scent of fresh rain on dry pavement. He wondered if loving her could wash away everything that had happened. Could they ever be clean of it? He drifted off.

———

Eve was bound in the darkness of a small cement room. Will untied her. They were both covered in blood. An ax rested on the floor next to the body of a dead man dressed in a fine suit. A dark pool of blood spread from his head.

———

Will looked out the rear window of the bus. His father stood illuminated in the cool white of a streetlight. The royal color of his uniform glowed in the dark night, a blue beacon getting smaller and smaller.

I can't stop thinking about it, Dad.

Close off that part of your mind. You'll be better off.

Is that what you do? Will asked. You shut off your mind?

Sometimes, he said. Shut off your mind. Shut off your heart.

———

When Will woke, the lights were off and Eve was gone. He reached over and switched on the lamp.

There was a note in Eve's tiny, crooked writing sitting on the pillow next to him.

We're drawing too much attention.

Nigel can't keep his mouth shut.

See for yourself.

Will grabbed his phone and looked up *Beatty's Beat*. There on the front page was a shot of Will and Eve together at the diner.

"That asshole," he hissed.

Will skimmed the story. It was the usual garbage. Scandal, murder, gold.

"Nigel, it's time you learned how to tell the truth," Will muttered.

———

The *Hope News* headquarters was in a tiny building next to a warehouse at the center of town.

Will flung the door open and entered. He saw Nigel Beatty immediately. He was lounging in his office chair with his feet up on his desk.

A secretary who looked to be well past retirement age sat knitting nearby. There were no other employees present.

Nigel spotted Will at the last moment. He made a clumsy attempt to stand, but Will pulled him up by the collar and threw him against a filing cabinet.

"Now wait, hold on," Nigel stammered. "We haven't seen each other in years. Why don't we go get a drink and catch up?"

Will gave him another shove.

Nigel winced. He wasn't a fighter. Will had seen him get his ass kicked plenty of times in school by the rougher local kids. But what Nigel lacked in muscle he made up for in smarts and a quick mouth.

"I can help," Nigel said. "I have ways of getting information. If you've been digging around, then you know something doesn't smell right."

"Don't fuck with me," Will whispered. He wanted

to hit him, but he took a deep breath and released him.

Nigel shrugged it off as best he could, straightening his button-up shirt and glasses. "You can't be mad at me for writing the news," he said. "It's a small town, remember? You're the one who came back. You're kind of hard to ignore."

"I had to come back!" Will shouted, his stress getting to him. "And why I'm here is none of your business."

"No, Will," said Nigel. "It *is* my business." He pulled a bottle out of the desk drawer, offering it to Will.

Will shook his head.

Nigel took a swig himself. "When you left and no one knew where you went, it was…it was hard on a lot of people. Not just your dad. Or Eve. I have to say, man, I took it personally. We were like brothers."

"Would a brother write stories that say I took a bunch of gold and ran?"

Nigel held up his hands. "It's what everyone was thinking."

Will sat down in Nigel's chair. He was so tired. "You know, I was kind of looking forward to seeing you again one day," he said.

"Me too," said Nigel.

"And then I saw that video of my dad's dead body on your website," said Will in a deadly voice.

"That video—" Nigel began.

"Where did you get it?" Will asked.

"It was sent to me anonymously."

"Yeah, right."

"I can't reveal my sources, Will, but for this—for you—I would. But I don't know who sent me the link."

"No idea where it came from?"

Nigel shrugged. "I tried everything. There was no way to trace it. I turned it over to the cops."

"Which cops?" asked Will.

"Rivers," said Nigel. "But since it was death by suicide, he figured it didn't matter. He thinks Aaron Sullivan sent it."

"Why?" Will asked. "Wouldn't that make him a suspect?"

"Or Aaron did it to flush you out," said Nigel. "You've been away, and no one knew where you were. Hell, Rivers couldn't even find you, and I know he tried."

"Well, I'm back. And it looks like someone did kill my dad."

"How?" Nigel asked.

"Poison," said Will. "But no one knows that yet."

"And you're telling me?" Nigel asked.

Will smirked. "I want a favor."

"Name it," he said.

"Get that information to the right person. Reveal it like a scoop. But don't say where you got it from." Will took a piece of paper from Nigel's desk and wrote down a name. He folded it and handed to Nigel. "Open it when I'm gone."

Nigel nodded, and the two sat in silence, looking at each other.

"Fall back in love with her yet?" Nigel asked finally.

"I never stopped," said Will. "And do me another favor, okay? You stay away from Eve. The last thing she needs is you bringing up the past again."

"Because you're doing a great job of that yourself?" asked Nigel.

Will couldn't argue with that. Nigel was usually right, and that pissed him off.

"I was going to get in and get out," said Will. "But now things are all fucked up."

They sat in silence.

"When's the funeral?" Nigel asked at last.

"Few days. I have things to do first. To prepare."

"Listen, I can do some digging if you want. But I have to know what I'm digging for."

"Sulfur," Will said.

"I was hoping you wouldn't say that."

Will shrugged and got up to leave. "I need to look for a connection to Hell's Gate. A fun new drug. Ask around."

"I've heard of it," Nigel said. He thought for a moment. "You know what you're doing, right, Will?"

Will didn't answer. He just walked out.

Chapter Eleven

Will waited outside the Armory pub for over an hour. Finally a burgundy Ford Tempo blasting rock music pulled up to the curb.

Nigel was at the wheel, and Toby was in the passenger seat. He was drinking from a large bottle of vodka.

"Christ," said Will. "Took you long enough. I thought we were going to talk business."

"Look, dude, I'm sorry," said Toby. "I figured we could have some fun first." He laughed. Clearly he was drunk.

Will was not impressed. "What's he doing here?" Will asked, motioning to Nigel.

"Aw, come on," said Toby. "You guys still mad at each other?"

"Hey, I'm cool if he is," said Nigel.

"Will?" Toby asked. "Look, just come back to my place. I have the dopest dope. Promise it'll be epic. Like the old days."

Will thought for a moment. "What the hell."

Toby hooted in celebration. "That's what I'm talking about!"

Will looked around, then got into the back seat, and the car pulled away.

———

Toby's house was in the forest, down a long stretch of gravel road. Cars and trucks lined the drive, and loud heavy-metal music came from inside.

Locals in their late teens and early twenties filled the small kitchen. It was a crowd of jean jackets and plaid. The kitchen counter overflowed with empty beer bottles and half-full liquor bottles. A yellow plastic bucket stamped with the SulCorp logo sat beside the fridge. It was completely filled with bottle caps. The group was having a great time, already riled up.

Will leaned against the kitchen door frame. He was the only one without a drink in his hand. He checked his watch.

"Where did Toby go?" he asked, but no one answered him.

Nigel was at the center of the throng, a girl in each arm. He saw Will standing alone.

"Hey! Someone loosen that guy up," shouted Nigel.

Will shot him a look.

Toby came into the room, grabbed a beer and brought it over to Will.

Will shook his head.

"It's a party, Will," said Toby. "Remember the concept?"

"Yeah, but that's not why I'm here."

"Lighten up, man. We can talk business later."

Will thought for a moment. "Got anything stronger?"

"What? Like whiskey?"

"Stronger."

"I'm afraid you're going to have to be more specific, old friend. I mean, I have to be sure you won't go tattling on me. Not that the cops in this town give me much trouble."

"Got something that'll make me forget who I am?" asked Will. "A pill, a powder, a kick to the head? I don't care. Send me to hell and back."

Toby smiled. "Now that's the spirit." He motioned for Will to follow.

Once outside, Toby, Nigel and the girls all crowded around the firepit as Will started a fire.

"Would you look at that?" said Nigel. "The Boy Scout strikes again."

Will stood. "Screw you."

"Now, now, children," said Toby. "We came here to have a good time. And our Boy Scout friend here had the genius idea to take this party to the next level. So we should all thank the Boy Scout."

"Thanks, Boy Scout!" they all shouted together.

"So what's the drug?" Will asked.

Toby pulled a baggie filled with yellow pills from the inner pocket of his jean jacket. "A little something."

The girls held out their hands, not caring what it was.

"What the hell is it?" asked Nigel.

"Exactly. Hell indeed," said Toby.

Will stepped forward to look at the product. "What's in it?"

"It's a secret formula."

"Where did you get it?" asked Nigel.

"Jesus," said Toby. "You two with the questions. You want to get high or not?"

"Sure, but I don't want it to kill me," Nigel said.

"Don't worry. I'll go first." Toby grabbed a yellow capsule and swallowed it dry. "See?"

Toby doled out caps to them all.

"Can I have two?" asked one of the girls.

"Now, now. These are like Wonka's Everlasting Gobstoppers. You only need one, and that's all you're gonna get." When he got to Will, he placed the cap in his hand and looked him in the eye. "So don't go selling my secrets to old Slugworth now, you hear?"

Will smiled and popped the cap in his mouth. "Would I do that?"

"I don't know. Would you?" asked Toby.

"My Boy Scout days are long gone," said Will.

Toby grinned. "Welcome back to the dark side, my friend. To the *ex*-Boy Scout!"

"The *ex*-Boy Scout!" everyone shouted.

They all raised their beers and toasted Will.

———

Will wandered in the eerie woods as the moonlight, blue and cold, glinted off the wet leaves. He stood in the light drizzle and looked up at the sky. He didn't blink. He didn't care that rain was falling into his open eyes and running down his cheeks. He shivered and looked back through the trees.

The firepit was visible through the trees. Toby, Nigel and the girls were staring into it.

Though Will was less than twenty feet from the flicker of the orange fire, it appeared to him to be at the end of a long tunnel.

Nigel got up from his seat by the fire, turned in Will's direction and started walking toward him.

Nigel's movements were slow. Blue traces of light followed him.

He reached into his shirt pocket, pulled out a cigarette and lit it. Sparks flew from the point of ignition, first orange and then red, purple and blue.

Will blinked as if to clear his eyes—or as if to clear a memory from his mind. He began talking to himself.

"What do I do? I should get on a bus. No one will know where I am."

Suddenly Nigel appeared in front of Will.

"Hey!" said Nigel. "Snap out of it." He snapped his fingers, and Will blinked again, coming back to reality.

"Wh-what?" he said.

"Man, you are tripping," said Nigel.

"Aren't you?" Will asked.

"Hell no," said Nigel. "I wouldn't just take some pill Toby gave me. I figured I'd wait and see what it did to everyone else first. Besides, I never get high when I'm breaking a story."

"Huh?" Will asked.

Nigel eyed Will. "How come you took it? I thought you were trying to get a lead."

"Shut up," Will said. "I don't need these guys thinking I'm a narc."

Toby called out, "Hey, you guys! Come back!" He hurled an empty beer bottle at them, and it smashed against a tree.

Will leaned away to avoid the flying glass and fell over.

Nigel helped him up. "Come on, Will, let's go sit down a while." Nigel grabbed hold of his arm, but Will shook him off.

"It's like Eve said," he said, holding back tears. "Life is a series of landslides. It all comes down at once and crushes everything."

Nigel sighed. "You know, that's getting pretty old."

"What is?"

"I had to listen to you whine about Eve when we were kids. Now that you're back, I've got to listen to it some more?"

"Jeez," said Will. "Sorry."

Nigel shook his head. "You don't get it. I'm going to end up alone. It's not like there's too many decent girls around here anymore. I'm not ever going to have that forever love like you do."

Will blinked. "You could leave Hope, you know."

"Nah," Nigel said. "I have my mom to look after."

"Yeah," Will said softly. "You always were a good son. Better than me."

"Hey," said Nigel. "Don't be so hard on yourself. Look, let's go back to the fire, okay? Come on."

Will stumbled to the firepit with Nigel's help.

"Aw," Toby said, laughing. "They made up! Glad to see you're finally having a good time. Who'd have known that it would only take experimental drugs to do it?"

This last comment set the group around the fire into fits of giggles—all except for Nigel.

"What's that?" Will slurred. He pointed to some figures moving in the shadows beyond the circle of firelight.

One of the figures was small and dark. As Will stared, the figure walked into a slice of moonlight. It was Eve.

Will shook his head and closed his eyes. When he opened them again, he saw another figure, this one taller and darker. Aaron Sullivan.

Will lurched toward them but fell face-first into the dirt. The group giggled even harder.

Nigel crouched to help Will up.

"Stop it, Nigel!" Will shouted.

Nigel gave Toby a dirty look. "Your drugs really messed him up."

"It's old Slugworth himself," Will slurred. "And he has my girl." Will pointed.

Toby followed his gaze. "Sullivan!" he shouted, as he made a beeline for the house.

Aaron and Eve were standing near the house, illuminated by the porch light. Toby hurried to them, shook Aaron's hand and took them in through the back door.

"Son of a bitch," Nigel breathed.

Will threw up into the fire and then fell backward.

Nigel kneeled beside him and placed a hand on his chest. "Welcome back to Hope, Will. I may not be able to leave, but I'll do everything I can to get you out of here."

Chapter Twelve

Will dreamed about walking on an endless highway bathed in blue moonlight. As he walked, sex workers beckoned to him. Each one of their faces turned into Eve's. He went to them, and they disappeared into the night air.

He woke up on a deflating air mattress in a bedroom filled with storage boxes, tools and exercise equipment. The house was quiet, except for some muffled conversation in the hallway.

Will sat up and noticed that someone was standing in front of the closed door, staring at him. It was Eve.

"Eve, what—"

"Don't talk," she said, interrupting him. "Listen."

She walked closer. "It was a mistake to get together again," she said.

"Don't," Will pleaded. "Don't do this."

"It's too risky," she said. "We'll blow it. And then I'll be nothing to you. Another bag of bones turning tricks on the highway."

Will was quiet for a moment before looking up into her eyes. "Why am I always losing you?"

Eve sat down next to him. "We can't draw so much attention. Do what you came here to do and then leave. Or forget it all and leave tonight. Things are getting too fucked up."

"Why? What's happened? Did Aaron do something?"

"No. I'm feeling a lot of heat is all," she said.

"Then I'll make it stop," said Will.

Eve placed a hand on his cheek. "Leave, Will," she whispered. "Leave Hope. Leave me. You did it once. You can do it again."

Will shook his head and took her hand in his. "I can fix it. Don't you see that by running away I ruined everything? My life, yours, my father's. Now is my chance to make it right."

She shook her head. "There are some things you can't change. And I'm one of them. You should know that by now."

"I know that I love you."

Eve stared at him, a look of fear on her face. "Loving me could get you killed."

She got up and walked to the door. She opened it into the bright hallway, where Aaron was waiting.

She walked away, brushing past Aaron as she went.

Aaron walked toward him. "This town isn't your fix-it project, Will," he said. "Its problems are my inheritance."

"I'm going to make things right," Will answered.

"Always the hero. Be careful."

Nigel appeared in the doorway behind Aaron. "Nice suit," he said. "You get that at Dirtbags 'R' Us?"

Aaron scoffed. "Move aside, paper boy," he said. He walked back down the hall toward a nervous-looking Toby.

"You should be more careful of the company you keep," Aaron said to him.

"Come on, man," said Toby. "Will is an old friend."

"Oh yeah? Well, his friends have a way of getting themselves hurt," Aaron warned. "Especially if those friends don't keep certain information to themselves. Know what I mean?"

Toby took a step back. "Yeah, man. I got it."

Aaron left, moving as quickly and quietly as a cat.

Will got up and walked to the door. He was a bit wobbly on his feet, and Nigel put out an arm to steady him.

"Thanks," said Will.

"No problem. What are friends for, huh?"

Will looked at him for a long moment. "You sure you want to be a friend to me?" he asked at last. "Like the man said, it's a dangerous job."

Nigel shrugged. "Yeah, well, I can handle it."

"Famous last words," said Will.

"Oh, hey," said Nigel. "While you were sleeping, you got a call from someone named Aunt Justine."

"Did you answer it?" Will asked, checking his phone. There was no message.

"No, I didn't," said Nigel. "But I thought your whole family was dead. Is that who you were staying with when you were away? An aunt of yours?"

Will ignored him and changed the subject. "Can you give me a ride?"

"Sure. Where to?" Nigel asked.

"I have to go bury my dad."

"Oof," said Nigel. "Can we stop for coffee first?"

"I wouldn't have it any other way," said Will.

Will grabbed his jacket from the bed and the two left, with Will leaning on his friend.

Chapter Thirteen

At the Hope cemetery, Will stood beside an open grave as his father's casket was lowered into the ground. Next to his father's temporary marker was an older tombstone with the name Beth Homer engraved on it. The epitaph read *Loving wife and mother.*

Rivers and Nigel stood next to Will. There were only a few other mourners—some retired cop friends and Dave from the morgue. He nodded to Will.

As the casket reached the bottom of the grave, Rivers placed a hand on Will's shoulder.

Will shrugged him off.

"I'm going to make you proud," Will whispered. He turned and looked Rivers in the eye. "Whoever did this is going to die."

"Will, be careful," said Rivers. "You are talking to a cop, remember?"

"How could I forget?" Will said, anger dripping from his voice.

"Will," said Nigel. "Come on, man."

Rivers pointed at Nigel. "Do me a favor, Beatty. Keep an eye on the kid, huh?"

"He can handle himself," said Nigel. "But don't worry. I got his back."

"You're gonna be the death of me, kid," said Rivers as he stepped away.

"Hey, Will," said Nigel, "who does Rivers like for this? Does he have a suspect?"

"Aaron Sullivan, of course," Will spat.

Nigel pointed to the road. "Speak of the devil."

A slick black BMW with a SulCorp hood ornament rolled up to the curb and stopped beside Rivers. The window was down, and there appeared to be a conversation taking place.

"You want to leave it up to him?" Nigel asked. "Or do you want to dig deeper?"

"Do you know something?" asked Will.

"Yeah," said Nigel. "There's something you need to see."

———

Nigel and Will stood in the living room of Nigel's house, where his mother, Edith, sat in a wheel-chair. She was crocheting a gigantic blue scarf.

"Hey, Mom," said Nigel. "I brought company."

Edith looked up. "Oh," she said. "Aren't you a sight for sore eyes!"

"I'll be right back," said Nigel. "I have some stuff I want you to see." He walked out of the room.

"Will," said Edith, "come here." She opened her arms.

Will walked over and bent down to kiss her on the cheek.

"It's so good to see you, Eddie," said Will.

"I only wish it were under better circumstances," she said. "Honey, I'm so sorry about your dad."

Will nodded. "I guess I'm an orphan now, huh?"

Edith shook her head. "Not so long as you've got us, honey. I know it's been strange. But you're like a brother to Nigel. You will always have a home here."

Will swallowed hard. It was true. Despite the bad history, Nigel was a true friend. One of the best he'd ever had.

Nigel walked back in carrying a blue file folder.

"I would have come to the funeral, but I wasn't feeling too well," said Edith. "My diabetes, you know." She pointed to where her left foot should have been.

"God, Eddie, I'm sorry," said Will. "When did that happen?"

"Oh, it's okay, honey. Nigel takes good care of me."

"Nah," said Nigel. "It's she who takes care of me, actually."

Will looked at the two of them. Their closeness hit him in the chest. He could have been here to help them out. Instead he'd been running from his problems, obsessed with ideas of revenge. All while his best friend was here, taking care of his sick mom alone. He should have known. Nigel's mom had had him late in life—all on her own— and then she had been plagued with bad health.

"I wish—" Will couldn't continue. He looked at Nigel. "You turned out okay, huh? Head of the paper, your own website, taking care of your mom."

Nigel shrugged. "What else was I going to do around here? Work in sulfur? No thanks."

Nigel smiled, but Will could see the sadness behind it. If anyone could have escaped this town, it would have been Nigel. He was the smart one. He was the one who did the best in school, who had the ambition to leave and make something of himself.

"Well," said Edith. "You've grown into such a handsome young man. I always thought you looked more like your mother, bless her soul. She was such a kind woman."

"I feel like I didn't know her," said Will. "I was a little kid when she died. And now..." He trailed off. It wasn't like his dad was around to keep the memories alive for him. Will felt like a train running off a crooked track. A train headed straight for disaster.

"How well can one person know another?" asked Edith. "When you were young, you were such a happy kid. Both you and Nigel were always running about and getting into adventures. No wonder my Nigel turned out to be a reporter."

"Mom," said Nigel. "Will's been through a lot."

"I know, honey. I can see it in his eyes."

Will nodded. "The past isn't in the past. My home isn't my home. My father..." Will was too choked up to continue.

"It's okay," said Nigel.

"I don't know what I'm doing here anymore," said Will, crying now.

Edith leaned forward and took Will's hand. "Everything is going to be okay."

Will took a deep breath and nodded.

A while later Nigel and Will sat at the kitchen table, eating grilled cheese sandwiches. Nigel opened a blue file folder stuffed with documents. He spread the papers out on the table. There were maps, land surveys, old court filings, obituaries and even a copy of the police report of Old Man Sullivan's death.

"You've been busy," Will said. "Did you only just start looking at this stuff?" He reached out and sifted through the pile, pausing on a photograph of Eve from years earlier.

Nigel shook his head. "I've been collecting things since you left town. There are benefits to working at the paper and knowing how to find things. Did you know that all of this"—he pointed to a legal document with a SulCorp logo on it—"is public record? Once these get filed in a court of law, anyone can read them."

Will nodded. "Anything good?"

"I found something interesting," Nigel said. He pulled out a photocopied sheet. "This says that Old Man Sullivan had a child with an unidentified woman. He had his lawyers draw up a plan to provide for the kid. I wanted to see if there might be some kind of connection to his murder. I mean, wouldn't Aaron have a reason to want to keep that information hidden? You know, for his inheritance?"

"I don't know," said Will. "I thought the mill was in financial trouble."

"That's the thing," said Nigel. "Their public financial statements show huge losses. But the mill keeps going. I can't figure out why Aaron Sullivan hasn't just pulled the plug. Why keep it open?"

Will stared at the papers. This was all so overwhelming. It was time to come clean to his friend.

"Will?" Nigel asked. "Are you listening?"

"It's nothing new," Will said at last.

"What do you mean?" asked Nigel.

"I'm saying," said Will, "that it's old news."

Nigel absorbed this for a moment, stunned. "Oh my god," he said at last. "Do you know who it is?"

Will was silent. "There's only so much I can tell you."

Nigel thought some more. "What are you planning, Will? And why are you even telling me this now?"

"Because I need a witness," Will said. "After it's all over. Someone who can finally tell the truth. And there is no one better for this than you. You know me. You know everyone involved. And you can get the information to a big audience."

Nigel looked worried. "What do you mean 'when it's over,' Will? Is this some kind of revenge against SulCorp? Don't do it, Will. Think about it. You'll get yourself killed. SulCorp owns this town. It owns the police."

Will shook his head. "Not my dad. They never owned him. Never."

"True," said Nigel. "But he might have been the only cop not in Old Man Sullivan's pocket."

Will smiled. "You've got it all wrong," he said. "So very wrong."

Nigel shook his head. "I don't understand."

Will took a deep breath. "You will when the plan is complete."

"There's a plan?" Nigel asked.

"There's always been a plan."

Nigel shoved the rest of his sandwich in his mouth. "Man, I missed you."

"Tell me that when this is all over," said Will. "For now, I need your help."

"Name it."

Chapter Fourteen

Nigel's Ford Tempo sat overlooking the river-
bank next to the mill. Rain poured down on
the windshield, too fast for the wipers to clear
it away.

A SulTrain came rattling by on the tracks
in front of them, a faint cloud of yellow dust
shaking off it.

Nigel smoked his cigarette down to the filter. He jammed the butt into the overflowing ashtray. Fast-food containers, clothes and gadgets littered the car.

"What is all this junk?" asked Will.

"Junk? This is how I make a living," said Nigel. He held up a tiny microphone and slipped it under his shirt. "For recording," he said.

"Wow, so you're a real supersleuth, huh?" teased Will.

"Need evidence," said Nigel. "And insurance."

"Insurance?"

"This mic is wireless. It's connected to my server back at the office. I set it to auto upload every night at midnight. It will go live on my website and to all my contacts unless I cancel it."

"Smart," said Will.

"Safe, more like it," said Nigel. "I don't want to end up in the sulfur—" He stopped. "Sorry. I should have thought before I said that."

"It's okay," said Will. "Make me a copy of whatever you get."

Nigel nodded. He pointed at the railcar. "I swear this whole town and everything in it smells like that rotten stuff. It never goes away."

"Like the smell of death," said Will.

Nigel gave him a look.

"Do you think sulfur is all they ever transport in those railcars?" Will asked.

"Only one way to find out," Nigel said as he opened his car door.

A few minutes later the two of them crouched near the mill's perimeter fence.

Nigel pulled his phone out and started taking pictures.

The two of them slipped under a gap in the chain-link fence and shadowed their way over to the parked railcars.

Most of the cars were empty except for glowing yellow dust. One of the lines of cars started moving, and they jumped on board. It tracked along the yard until it reached the SulCorp loading area, then came to a stop.

"What now?" Nigel whispered.

"We wait," said Will.

"For what?"

Will didn't answer and instead nodded toward the main office building.

As they watched, the door opened and Aaron Sullivan walked out. A goon followed along with two snarling blue-eyed dogs. He gave them to Aaron, who took a leash in each hand.

Workers in coveralls carried out small rectangular packages. They packed them into larger boxes and then placed them into the small carrier cars as they inched by.

"Faster, boys," called out Aaron in the distance.

"We've got a deadline to meet. And besides, I have a date tonight." He laughed, the sound mingling with the train sounds until it was nearly the same noise.

As each car advanced forward, packed to the hilt with boxes, a large funnel deposited a fine plume of sulfur on top.

"I knew it," said Nigel. "It has to be the drugs. They must be moving millions here." He snapped a few photos. "Man, when I break this story, it's going to get picked up by the national outlets."

A voice came from behind them. "That ain't the only thing you're gonna break," said the goon. He grabbed Nigel by the collar and hauled him from the railcar.

When Will made a move to help him, the goon pulled a gun. Will stopped, but his own hand inched toward the gun hidden in his waistband.

"Easy," said Will. "We don't want trouble."

Aaron walked up with his growling dogs. "Well," he said. "You found it."

Nigel and Will exchanged a look.

"We're screwed," whispered Nigel.

"Come along now," said Aaron. "We'll be much more comfortable in my office."

The goon released Nigel and motioned for them to follow after Aaron.

Inside the mill office, Will and Nigel sat across from Aaron, who glared at them from behind his desk.

"Tell me why I shouldn't call the cops," said Aaron.

Nigel cleared his throat. "Uh…because you have a shitload of drugs moving through your railyard?"

"I do?" asked Aaron with a wry smile.

Nigel looked confused, but Will was calm and expressionless. He watched Aaron closely.

"You're looking in the wrong place," said Aaron.

"Then what's in those boxes?" asked Nigel. He nodded to the small rectangular containers stacked behind Aaron.

Aaron let loose a rasping laugh. "Those are parts, paper boy."

Nigel raised an eyebrow. "Body parts?"

Aaron rolled his eyes. "No. They're bolts, idiot." He grabbed a box and opened it, dumping it out onto his desk. Sure enough, a pile of steel bolts rolled out. "We started manufacturing and selling bolts on the side. Times are tough. Gotta diversify."

"Tough times?" said Nigel. "What about your inheritance? That legendary Sullivan gold?"

"Not this again," Aaron muttered.

"The drugs," said Nigel. "Hell's Gate is a sulfur compound."

"An unfortunate coincidence," Aaron said.

"Well, if not you, then who?" asked Nigel.

"That's what I was thinking you could help with," said Aaron. "The drug is bad for business. People dying all over the place. Turning up in my sulfur piles. Much as I don't care for the Homers," he said, nodding toward Will, "at the same time, I don't like finding them dead at my mill."

"Wait," said Will. "You found him? My dad?"

"Poetic, isn't it?" said Aaron. "You found my dad. And I found yours."

There was a heavy silence in the room.

The phone rang, cutting through the tension. Aaron answered it and then was silent for a long moment before hanging up without a word.

"Sorry," he said. "It was my aunt."

Nigel gave him a puzzled look and glanced at Will. "I thought—" he began, but Will interrupted him.

"We should go," Will said.

"Now hold on," said Aaron. "I'd like to give you an exclusive, paper boy." He stared at Will. "Do you vouch for him, Will?"

Will looked at Nigel. "I do," he said. "You can trust him."

"Good," said Aaron. "Now, Will, kindly get the hell off my property."

"Fine," said Will. He got up to go.

"Meet me at the pub after," said Nigel. "We'll talk to Eve."

"A girl like Eve always finds trouble," said Aaron as Will walked out. "Remember that."

"I couldn't forget if I tried," Will whispered.

He exited through the main gate, under the watchful eye of the goon.

Chapter Fifteen

Will and Nigel slid into a corner booth in the Armory pub, away from the crowded bar and the nearby pool tables.

"Well, that was fucking weird," Nigel said.

"Which part?" Will asked. "Everything is weird about this."

"Good point," said Nigel. "I guess I just wasn't

expecting to hear all of that. Least of all from Aaron Sullivan."

"Did you get everything you needed?" Will asked.

"More," said Nigel. "So much more."

Sam the barman lumbered over to their table, interrupting them. "You guys drinking?"

"No," said Will.

"Then get the hell out so I can give this table to paying customers."

"Aw, come on, Sam. We came by to see your boyfriend," said Nigel.

Sam shrugged. "He isn't here. Should be though. He promised he'd help me change over some kegs. He's not answering his phone either. If it wasn't so busy, I'd zip home and haul his cute ass back here, but we're slammed. Can you guys can track him down?"

"Sure," said Will. "Hey, have you seen Eve?"

Sam shook his head. "She didn't show up for her shift. Come to think of it, those two better not be off somewhere getting high together."

Will and Nigel exchanged a look.

"What?" asked Sam. "Do you guys know something? You better spill it." He leaned forward, his thick arms resting on the table and sending a clear message.

"No," said Will. "But we'll let you know if we find them."

Will and Nigel hurried out.

"If you do find them," Sam called after them, "tell my boyfriend he's in trouble."

———

Nigel sped through town to the outskirts. When he turned onto the gravel road to Toby's house, blue flashes of light peeked through the woods.

Nigel pulled over next to a police car. There was an ambulance idling beside it.

"Shit," said Will. He jumped out of the car and hurried up the front steps to the open door.

He stared down the hall. It was dark save for occasional flashes from a police photographer's camera. The flashing stopped, and someone flipped on the overhead light switch.

Nigel gasped beside him and turned away, but Will stepped forward. He'd seen this kind of thing before.

There was blood all over the walls and the carpet leading down the hall. At the end, in the doorway, lay Toby. He had slashed wrists, and his face was blue. EMTs were tending to him, fitting him with an oxygen mask and trying to stop the bleeding.

"Oh my god. Oh my god," said Nigel.

Will turned to him. "You have to call Sam. Right now."

Nigel nodded and pulled out his phone.

The EMTs loaded Toby onto a stretcher and rushed him through the door. As they passed Nigel and Will, Toby groaned, and his eyes fluttered.

"Toby!" said Will. He took a step to follow, but a cop blocked his path.

"Whoa, where do you think you're going?" the cop asked.

"That's my friend," said Will. "I want to make sure he's okay."

"Your friend? Well, he's got himself in a pickle, all right. First he's got to survive, and then he's got to answer for all the drugs we found in this house. Know anything about that?"

Will shook his head. "I'm looking for my girlfriend, Eve Hart." He swallowed a lump that had formed in his throat. "Is she…is she here?" He was struck with a deep fear that she was also injured—or worse.

The cop shook his head. "No, but we'd like to speak to her too. In the meantime, you are trespassing on a crime scene. Leave before I throw you in the clink."

"I'm a member of the press," said Nigel, stepping forward and showing his press card.

The cop rolled his eyes. "Well, I have a badge too, and that badge says you need to go."

Will flinched, a memory flooding back to him of a time after he'd left town. He had called his dad, wanting to talk to him, but he couldn't get any words out. Instead he'd cried while listening to his dad say, "Hello?" over and over.

"We'll go," said Will. "But is Detective Rivers here? He's...kind of my uncle."

"Oh yeah? Jim's one of the best," said the cop. "He went looking for that girlfriend of yours. Seems she was the last person seen with our drug dealer here."

"Shit," said Nigel.

They turned and walked back toward the car. "We have to find her first," said Will.

"Damn, Will," said Nigel as they got into his car. He bit the nails on his left hand as he started the Tempo and began to drive. "Do you think Toby will be okay? Sam was so freaked on the phone. And will he go down for a long time? And Eve too?"

"Nigel, calm down. There's more to this," said Will. "Toby wouldn't do this to himself."

"I know. He was so happy with Sam." Nigel sighed. "This is all connected. I know it now. I mean, after Aaron told me everything…" He shot a look at Will.

Will nodded. "I know. Stay the course, Nigel. It will all work out."

"It was so fucked up," said Nigel, a tremor in his voice. "Man, I knew you had a plan, but wow. This is big."

"I have to go all the way," said Will. "You'll understand when it's over."

Nigel let out a breath.

"We have to find Eve before Rivers does," said Will. "He can't find her first."

"This doesn't feel right," said Nigel. "It feels too much like..." He trailed off.

"It feels like the first time she went missing," said Will, completing Nigel's thought. "I know exactly where she is," he said.

———

Nigel's car pulled up to the SulCorp perimeter fence, and Will hopped out. He leaned in through the open window and shook hands with Nigel. He handed him his phone.

"Aaron told you what to do," Will said. "And you'll call Aunt Justine?"

"I'm solid," said Nigel.

"After that you stay away, okay?" Will said. "It's not safe."

"Yeah, man. Got it," said Nigel.

Will nodded and turned to go, but Nigel called after him. "Hey, Will!"

"Yeah?"

"Just, uh…" Nigel cleared his throat. "Be careful, okay? I don't want to lose you twice, man."

Will looked at his friend for a moment, nodded, then left as Nigel's car pulled back onto the highway.

Will walked up to the fence and grabbed the chain link. He climbed over and landed on the other side. He crouched behind a railcar and watched the yard. It appeared deserted. The shadows were deep and dark. He thought back to that awful night, how he'd cased this very place, looking for a way in.

———

He made his way down the hall and noticed a few drops of blood on the floor. They led to a stairwell. There was a room at the bottom. The door was ajar.

He looked inside. So much blood.

Old Man Sullivan lay murdered, hacked to death with an ax. Eve was bound in the corner. Thick blood seeped toward her in a growing puddle.

Will ran to her, slipping in the blood. He rushed to untie her.

"I knew you'd come," she said.

———

Will shook off the bad memory. "Nigel," he whispered. "I hope you're making that phone call."

He pulled his father's gun from the waistband of his jeans before slinking around to the main office. He crouched under the window where the blue light from security screens glowed through. The window was open a crack. He peeked in.

Aaron sat at his desk, a worried look on his face. Will followed his gaze, and his heart pounded in his chest when he saw the full scene.

The goon was dead on the floor, a large bullet wound in the center of his chest. Next to him a girl cowered, her head covered by a SulCorp sack. A tiny tattoo peeked out from under her shirt collar. Eve. She struggled against the zip tie binding her hands.

A boot kicked her. "Sit still," said a voice. It was a voice Will would recognize anywhere.

Detective Jim Rivers.

Chapter Sixteen

Will shifted to see the corner of the room that was out of sight.

Rivers had a gun pointed at Eve's head.

"Any sign of our special friend?" Rivers asked Aaron.

"None," he said, pointing to the video monitors with bound hands.

"He'll come," said Rivers. "He won't be able to stay away. It's all too much like it was before."

Will looked at Eve. She sat very still, calm, upright. "Don't worry," Will whispered. "I won't make the same mistake again."

He paused for a moment and then hurried over to the office door. He kicked it in, gun drawn, but Rivers had the jump on him. Will felt the barrel of a handgun pressed to his temple.

"Easy, Uncle Jim," said Will.

"Perfect timing, kid," said Rivers. "Now take that gun, release the clip and kick it across the room."

Will did as he asked.

Aaron began to laugh.

"What's so funny?" Rivers demanded.

"You're a little early," said Aaron.

"I am?" asked Rivers.

"The big climax is yet to come," said Aaron.

"Stop the games," said Rivers. He pulled the sack off Eve's head. "Or I'll shoot her."

"Don't you touch her," said Will.

"Then give me what I want," said Rivers. "Just one thing."

"Name it," said Will.

"The map."

Will sighed. "I hoped it wasn't true for a long time, Uncle Jim. All this for money?"

Rivers frowned. "What? I don't deserve a shot at the Sullivan gold? After spending my whole life cleaning up the town? I'm old, Will. And I'm tired of the smell of this place. Now give me what I came for before you end up in a sulfur pile too."

Will shook his head. "That gold has blood on it," he said.

"The Sullivan fortune came from the gold rush days, so I'm sure there's plenty of blood on it," said Rivers. "What's a little more?"

"I can't help you," said Will. "Even if I wanted to, I don't know where it's hidden."

"But you can figure it out. Like your dear old dad did."

"No," said Will.

"Don't bullshit a bullshitter, kid. I know when someone is lying," said Rivers. "I knew your dad was lying. He was a stubborn old fool. I knew there was a map, but he wouldn't give it to me, and he wouldn't give up your location either. Hell, I couldn't even track you down with skip tracers. Your dad hid you well. Guess you all wanted that gold for yourselves."

Will's rage threatened to boil over. "So you killed him."

"I had no choice," Rivers said with an evil smile. "Killing him was the only way to get you to come back to town."

"I hate you," said Will. "You'll pay for this."

"No," said Rivers. "I don't think so. I'll get away with it. Just like I did when Old Man Sullivan refused to give up the gold. I cleaved his head in two with an ax, and I walked right on out of here."

"Goddamn you!" Aaron shouted, struggling against his bonds.

"I knew it was you," whispered Eve.

Rivers turned to look at her.

She continued talking quietly. "Mr. Sullivan gave me a job, you know? He was teaching me some office stuff. Keeping me off the streets. He was nice to me."

She looked at Aaron. "He wasn't the monster everyone made him out to be."

"I know," Aaron said, tears running down his cheeks now.

Eve continued. "That night, when I was walking here for my shift, a cop car pulled up on me. Blinded me with its spotlight. I thought I was going to get pulled in. I thought I was going to have to give some cop a favor. Before I knew it, I got cracked over the head with a flashlight."

Will swallowed hard. This part of the story was always so hard to hear.

"Next thing I knew," she said in a shaky voice, "I was waking up in a cold room with a bag over my head. I was tied up. I heard someone breathing. And then I felt…something warm and wet on the ground. And then you"—she looked at Will—"you came and saved me."

"Ever the hero," said Rivers. He waved his gun at Will. "If you hadn't shown up, poking your nose around, things would have been different. But you came, and then your meddling dad, and soon the place was crawling with Hope's finest."

"And my father was dead," said Aaron.

Rivers laughed. "Imagine. That old bag of bones died for her. She was the bait. I thought he'd hand over the gold. But when he saw her tied up, he went crazy. He attacked me. It was practically self-defense."

"You're vile," said Will.

"Enough with story time!" Rivers shouted. "Give me the map, goddammit! That gold is *mine*. I killed for it. And if you don't give it to me, you will die for it."

He pressed the cold barrel of his gun against Will's head.

"No!" Aaron shouted. He leaped up from his chair and lunged at Rivers.

Rivers spun and fired off a shot. The bullet hit Aaron in the shoulder, sending him staggering backward. He collapsed onto the office floor.

Aaron struggled. He tried to crawl away. "Please," he wheezed.

"That's what your daddy said when I killed him with his own ax," said Rivers. "And now I'm going to kill you." He aimed his gun.

"Stop!" Will screamed. "He's my brother! Please, Uncle Jim, please. Don't hurt him."

Rivers stared at him. "Your *what*?"

"It's me you want," said Will. "Shoot me. Not him."

"No, Will!" Aaron screamed.

Rivers laughed. "Of course," he said. "There was something that always bothered me about how much time you spent here. Why you were always around. It makes sense. And your mother, well, she got around. There were rumors. No wonder your dad drank so much."

"Stop," Will said. "You don't have to do any of this."

"Don't I?" asked Rivers. "Tell me," he said, leaning down over Aaron. "How long have you known you were brothers?"

"Long enough," gasped Aaron. "I found out right after you killed my dad." He stared at Rivers, the hatred obvious on his face.

"I found out after my mom died," said Will. "Old Man Sullivan started paying my way. He was good to me. And to my dad."

Rivers chuckled. "Well, isn't this sweet? It's going to make it so much better when you're all dead."

"Please," Will pleaded. "Just let them go."

There was a moment of silence when Rivers seemed to consider this. Finally he looked Will dead in the eyes and cocked his gun.

"No," he said. He pulled the trigger and a shot rang out, hitting Aaron in the chest.

Eve screamed, and Will fell to the floor. He couldn't tear his eyes from his brother. He crawled toward him to try to help. But Aaron was gravely hurt, the huge wound in the center of his chest pouring blood.

"No, no, no!" Will cried. "Aaron, wait. Hold on. Don't go."

Aaron sputtered and coughed. Blood sprayed from his lips. "Will," he croaked. "You have to finish it. Just burn it all down, bro. It's not worth it. Just get away."

"Tell me where the gold is, boy," said Rivers, crouching down next to him. "And I'll call an ambulance. You might still make it."

"Fuck you," Aaron wheezed.

"Wrong answer," said Rivers. He fired another shot, hitting Aaron in the temple.

Before Will could process what was happening, his brother was gone. There was no going back.

Chapter Seventeen

"Now," said Rivers, pressing his gun to the back of Will's head, "give me what I asked for. Your brother was stupid. Don't be like him."

"Stop," said Eve. "I'll take you to the gold."

"Eve, no!" Will shouted.

"There is a map," she said. "I *am* the map."

"You," said Rivers.

"He was like a father to me too," said Eve. "Mr. Sullivan was kind to me. And he showed me where the gold was. Said if anything ever happened to him, I should take it and run away—with his sons."

"Show me," said Rivers.

"I'll take you," said Eve. "But you can't hurt Will. You hurt him, and the deal is off."

Rivers chuckled. "Let's go." He pulled out a knife and cut Eve's ties before dragging them both to their feet. He led them at gunpoint out into the mill yard.

"This way," said Eve. She walked to the center of the yard and then took a hard right turn. She took them past the railcars and buildings and trucks to the long-term storage piles. Every now and then she looked up at the sky, as if she was using the stars to guide her. They stopped at a large pile in the northeast part of the grounds.

"In there," she said. "There's a chest."

"Dig it up," said Rivers. He shoved Will forward and kept the gun trained on them as they scooped sulfur away with their hands.

The yellow dust plumed around them, covering them both with a sickly veil. Finally Will's hands struck a hard surface. He pulled out a heavy trunk and dropped it in front of Rivers.

"Open it," said Rivers.

"There's no key," said Will, pointing to the heavy lock.

Rivers fired off a shot, and the bullet sparked blue flames on the sulfur-covered chest. The lock smoldered. He kicked it loose.

"Open it," he said again.

Will pried the lid up. It groaned open.

Rivers stepped forward and used his flashlight to peer inside.

There was only a tiny bundle resting there. He picked it up and unfolded it.

"You son of a bitch," said Rivers. In his hand he held a single gold piece. And something else too—William Homer's police badge.

Will smiled. "You get nothing," he said. "It's all gone."

Rivers's face twisted with rage. "Say good night," he said, raising his gun.

Suddenly a car screeched onto the grounds and raced toward them, its horn honking and lights flashing.

"Nigel!" Eve cried out.

Will grabbed Eve and dove out of the way as Nigel's car made contact with Rivers and sent him flying into the sulfur pile.

The Tempo idled, and Nigel rammed his hand on the horn. Then he flung open the door and jumped out with a shiny object in his hand.

"Nigel, no! Get back—"

But it was too late. Before Will could finish, Rivers emerged from the sulfur pile and opened fire.

Bullets sprayed the lot, pinging off the Tempo.

"Will, run!" Nigel yelled, and then he fell silent.

Nigel looked down at his stomach. He had been shot. He made eye contact with Will and then fell back, unconscious.

Will ran to him. "Nigel!"

Eve tried to rouse him, pressing her hands into his bleeding stomach. "Oh, Will," she cried. "It's bad, it's so bad."

"Will," Nigel sputtered as he coughed up blood. "I did it. I made the call. I set it up." He held out Will's phone.

"No," Will moaned. "You stupid bastard. I told you to stay away."

Nigel managed a weak smile. "I had to. I… needed to ask you."

"What?" Will asked.

"I needed to ask you what time it is," said Nigel, his smile widening.

Will blinked. "Oh," he said. He checked his

watch. "It's one minute to midnight."

"One minute," said Nigel. "I did it."

Rivers staggered over. The impact of the car had messed up his leg, but he still had the upper hand. "What's he saying?" Rivers demanded.

"One minute until your whole…world…ends." Nigel's eyes closed.

"Nigel?" Will shook him. "Nigel!"

"What did he mean?" Rivers shouted.

"At midnight this broadcasts live," said Will.

Rivers staggered backward. "W-what?"

Will lifted Nigel's shirt, revealing hidden wires. Then he lifted his own.

"You fucker," Rivers said. "You're recording this? Well, it won't do you any good now." He reached over and ripped the wires away.

"Doesn't matter," Will said. "Nigel's been recording us this whole time. Aaron was bugged for days. Me and Eve too. It's all linked to an offsite server."

"Then I'll destroy it," said Rivers.

"Too late," said Will. "It went live on the internet a few seconds ago. And to my contact at the FBI. They know everything. And they're coming."

Rivers shook his head, confused. "How?" he demanded.

"See for yourself," said Will. "Check Nigel's site." He picked up his phone and opened the browser.

Rivers snatched it from him and clicked the link, the horror on his face growing by the second. He threw the phone into the sulfur. "No!" he screamed.

"Like he said." Eve smiled. "Your whole world is about to end."

"And now you'll know how it feels," added Will.

"Don't worry, kid," said Rivers in a menacing tone. "There won't be anyone left alive who cares." He cracked Will on the head with the butt of his gun.

The image of Eve crying was the last thing Will saw. Then it all went black.

Chapter Eighteen

Nigel's Tempo rested on an incline at the top of the hill. It overlooked the sulfur mill and the whole town of Hope. The slide area, the motel, the Trainstop and the Armory all looked tiny. As night faded into day, a faint blue light appeared over the mountain.

Will struggled to stay awake.

Nigel slumped in the driver's seat. He was breathing in ragged puffs, but he was alive. A heavy brick lay on the gas pedal. The engine revved, but the car was still in Park.

The dead goon was in the passenger seat. Eve and Will were in the back. Eve was also unconscious, a nasty bruise on her head. Rivers must have knocked her out too.

Rivers opened up the back door, reached in and cut off the connector buckles for the seat belts.

He put his face next to Will's. "The bullets those two ate were a gift," he said. "Nothing like the horrible fiery crash you're about to experience. And anyway, I want you to watch her die."

"You won't get away with this," said Will in a thin voice. "Everyone knows everything now."

"Maybe so," said Rivers. "But at least you'll be dead." He chuckled. "You know, I blame myself. It's because I have such a big heart. I cared about you."

"Fuck you, Uncle Jim," Will whispered.

Rivers grinned. "I should have killed you back then. It's my only true regret."

Sirens sounded in the distance.

"Bye, kid. Have a nice ride." Rivers shut the door, reached in through the front window and put the car in gear.

The Tempo lurched forward and then picked up speed. It zoomed faster and faster, straight for the rockslide memorial at the bottom.

Will tried to shove Nigel out of the way to get to the brakes, but there was no getting past him. There was no time.

He turned to Eve and took his father's handcuffs from his boot. He used the cuffs to clip a seat belt around them both, attaching it to a metal loop between the seat and the backrest.

The Tempo swerved and shuddered, sending off sparks.

Will brushed Eve's hair back from her face and traced the tattoo on her neck. He pushed it down a tiny bit to read the word inked there. His name.

"I knew you loved me," he whispered to her. He reached out to stroke her cheek.

The Tempo hit a bump and took flight. It floated through the cool fall air like a burning rocket. Billows of steam rose from the hot engine. The peaceful moment of flight gave way to a shattering crash as the sedan slammed into the rocks.

Will and Eve hurtled forward, but the seat belt stopped them. The driver's airbag opened, saving Nigel from going through the window, but the goon crashed through. He sailed forward until he struck a large boulder spray-painted with a blue heart. His body slid into the hollow at the base of the rock.

Chapter Nineteen

Will woke in a hospital room. A woman in a crisp navy suit stood next to his bed, taking notes. Her name tag identified her as FBI Special Agent Justine Tia. A plastic baggie lay on the table next to her. Inside it was Will's father's badge.

"Aunt Justine," croaked Will. "Took you long enough."

Will wheeled around the hospital halls alone, peeking into doors.

He wasn't allowed in to see Nigel. He was in the ICU, and Will wasn't blood family.

Toby was recovering after surgery. Will felt guilty about Toby getting caught up in their revenge plot against Rivers. It was never the plan for him to get hurt, but they hadn't had much of a choice. It was Toby who'd dealt Hell's Gate to the town, though he had gotten it from Rivers and his crew of crooked cops. It was the drugs and the connection to Rivers that had helped Will and Aaron get the feds interested in their case. Toby couldn't have known that Rivers would use those same drugs to murder Will's dad. He would never have wanted it to happen.

Will found Eve sleeping in a room. The FBI had put a protective detail on her to keep her safe in case Rivers showed up. He was still missing.

Will wheeled in and watched her a while before leaving her a note. It said:

Wait for me a little longer.

———

Months later, as Will sat in a truck parked on the highway, he opened his tablet and looked up *Beatty's Beat*. There was a link with a new viral video called *Hope's Most Wanted.*

He clicked it, and a video of the FBI busting Rivers at a rural rest stop began to play. Agents closed in on his car as it idled. The car door swung open and Rivers came out shooting. He died in a hail of bullets, the blood pooling in a black puddle beneath him.

———

The SulCorp sulfur mill lay silent like a sleeping yellow beast. None of its machines operated. It was quiet except for the clink of a fence gate closing and the sound of footsteps running away.

Will and Eve sat at the rockslide memorial, on the boulder with the blue heart. Eve smiled as a cool light illuminated her face. Will kissed her. They looked out over the horizon at the huge piles of sulfur burning in the distance. SulCorp was on fire, the flames glowing blue and brilliant against the night sky.

"Did we just burn down your inheritance?" Eve asked.

Will shrugged. "Good riddance," he said. "I think we'll be all right." He nodded to a duffel bag at their feet. A glint of gold peeked from behind a gap in the zipper.

"Where to?" she asked.

"Anywhere but here."

They got into Will's truck and took off down the highway.

As the blue fire burned, Will imagined what the mill must look like from high above. If he could float up into the sky with Eve and look down, what would he see?

Not the big out-of-control fire. Not the emergency vehicles scrambling to put it out. Not the train snaking around the spot where his dad had died. Not the place his biological father, Old Man Sullivan, had tried to save Eve.

He wouldn't see the true hiding place for the money. Or the place his brother, his last blood family member, had died trying to save him.

From high up, and from far away, he'd only see a burning blue heart. Just the lopsided shape of a past that was finally dead and buried.

Acknowledgments

This book was created during a pandemic, a time when everyone was sad and everywhere was a little bit dark. I'm so grateful to everyone who has had a hand in bringing this book to life, including the entire Orca pod. If you're reading this now, you should know that I think you are amazing. A special thank-you to screenwriter Sara Graefe for her guidance and feedback all those years ago and for igniting my interest in writing noir fiction. Thank you to the town of Hope. Although this book truly isn't about you, I did borrow your perfect name and part of your history for this story. Thank you to my friends for being there, even when they couldn't really be there. And, as always, thank you to Robert and my children. You are the light that sees me through.

LOGAN USES
HER CAMERA TO
WORK THROUGH
THE LOSS OF
HER MOM.

"Tackles serious
topics with
sincerity."
—*Kirkus Reviews*

WILL JOINING
A PUNK BAND
HELP KALLIE
FIND HER
PURPOSE?

"A thoroughly
modern and realistic
love story."
—*Resource Links*

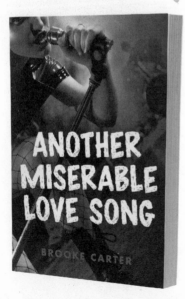

Brooke Carter is the author of several contemporary books for teens, including *Double or Nothing*, *Learning Seventeen* and *The Unbroken Hearts Club* from the Orca Soundings line.

orca soundings

For more information on all the books
in the Orca Soundings line, please visit

orcabook.com